Riley the Raccoon Goes to the Philippines

Written by Jasmine Arellano Montreuil
Illustrated by Chad Vivas

Tellwell Talent
www.tellwell.ca

ISBN
978-0-2288-4798-4 (Hardcover)
978-0-2288-4797-7 (Paperback)

For my loves:
Devin, Emerson and Bennett

Hi there!
My name is Riley the Raccoon.
Come and join me on a journey.
C'mon, I'm leaving soon!

His name is Tino the Tarsier;
he's a very good friend of mine.
He speaks Tagalog and English,
as well as American Sign.

He's going there to visit
his friends and family.
"You should come along!"
he suggested, excitedly.

Lola - Grandmother
Lolo - Grandfather
Tita - Auntie
Tito - Uncle
Pamangkin - Niece / Nephew
Apo - Grandson / Granddaughter

So, we're working on packing;
there are many things we need.
"Tino, are those gifts?"
"Yes! Chocolates, clothes, and books to read!"

"It's tradition to bring gifts
for those you visit there.
It's called pasalubong.
We have lots to prepare!"

"Salamat po" (Sah-lah-maht poh) means "thank you" in Tagalog. Po (Poh) is a sign of respect when talking to someone older than you.

Pasalubong (Pah-sah-loo-bong) is a homecoming gift.

"In the spirit of friendship,
honour, and giving,
our loving connection,
is what we're expressing."

"Maraming salamat po" (Mah-rah-meeng sah-lah-maht poh) means "thank you very much" in Tagalog.

"You bring a piece of home,
or if you're going somewhere new,
an interesting souvenir
for your loved ones too."

Now, we're on our way.
Beyond the clouds we go.
It's quite a long trip,
far away from winter's snow.

I start to draw a picture,
since waiting's hard for me,
of rice fields and mountains,
as far as I can see.

Est.
ARRIVAL
7 Hours

We're finally here.
Into the crowded jeepney we go.
Tino and I squeeze in,
with the pasalubong in tow.

Jeepney (Jeep-nee) is a common way of getting around in the Philippines.
Pasalubong (Pah-sah-loo-bong) is a homecoming gift.

We ride through the busy city,
then some countryside driving.
Then, THUMP, THUD, WHOA over a bump
and our luggage goes flying.

"Ay naku!"
Our luggage was no longer in view.
With all this heavy traffic,
deep inside Tino knew.

"Ay naku!" (Eye nah-koh!) means "Oh no!".

"The gifts are all gone.
We'll arrive empty-handed.
My Titos and Titas
will be so disappointed."

Titos (Tee-tohs) and *Titas (Tee-tahs)* means uncles and aunts.

"Huy! Kamusta ka na?"
His Lola greets us with a warm smile,
along with his Titos, Titas, Kuyas, and Ates,
and some friends he hasn't seen in a while.

"Huy! Kamusta ka na?" (Hooy! Kah-muhs-tah kah nah?) - Hey! How are you?
Lola (Loh-lah) means grandmother.
Titos (Tee-tohs) and Titas (Tee-tahs) means uncles and aunts.
Kuyas (Koo-yahs) and Ates (Ah-tehs) means older brothers and sisters.

She hugs both Tino and I,
and gives us a kiss, cheek to cheek.
She says, "Halika na!
Let's get something delicious to eat."

"Halika na!" (Hah-lee-kah nah!) means "Let's go!"

"We lost all the pasalubong."
"Ah ha, that's why the big frown.
The important thing is that we're together
and that you're here safe and sound."

Pasalubong (Pah-sah-loo-bong) is a homecoming gift.

They planned a big, colourful party,
and oh my, what a handa.
There's pancit, lumpia and turon.
Tino said, "Salamat po, ang ganda."

Turon (Too-rohn) – fried banana dessert

Lumpia (Loom-pya) – spring rolls

Handa (Hahn-da) is a spread of food for a celebration.

"Salamat po, ang ganda." (Sah-lah-maht poh, ahng gahn-dah) means "Thank you, it's beautiful."

Pancit (Pahn-seet) - noodles

Relieved, Tino squealed, "Yippee!
How kind of you to come all this way.
Maraming salamat, Carlo.
Please, will you join us and stay?"

Yippee!

Yippee!

Yippee!

"Maraming salamat" (Mah-rah-meeng
sah-lah-maht) means "Thank you very much"

"So, I used my horns to toss the luggage into my kalesa. Then, I used my nose to follow you to Lola Carmencita."

Kalesa (Kah-leh-sah) is a two-wheeled horse-drawn carriage.

Carlo was happy to join us,
for food, dancing, laughter, and song.
Now, finally it's time,
to hand out the pasalubong.

Pasalubong (Pah-sah-loo-bong) is a
homecoming gift.

A little surprise for each one,
how fun it is to see,
especially when the little ones
smile and yelp with glee.

We have lots of exciting plans
for the rest of our vacation,
but this will be my favourite memory
from this incredible nation.

Did you know that the Philippine tarsier is one of the world's smallest primates? Just like me, tarsiers are nocturnal, meaning they sleep all day and are awake all night. When they are awake, you can find them up high in the trees, trying to find their favourite food... BUGS! Though, you need to look hard, as the tarsier can be very shy. We need to take good care of the tarsier population, as there are not very many of them left in the wild and are considered endangered.

Tarsier

Meet the mighty carabao! Or kalabaw, they're called in Tagalog. The carabao is a type of water buffalo and a farmer's best friend here in the Philippines. Carabaos are very strong animals and are often found working, like ploughing rice fields. They even provide the family with fresh milk and cheese! Taking breaks are important, and working in hot and humid weather can be tough. Guess how they like to have fun and cool off? By rolling in the mud! These gentle giants are such a beloved part of Philippine heritage and culture, that the carabao is considered the National animal of the Philippines.

Carabao

Made in the USA
Las Vegas, NV
22 March 2022

46154917R00021